Lizzie
the Sweet Treats
Fairy

Special thanks to
Narinder Dhami

ORCHARD BOOKS
338 Euston Road, London NW1 3BH
Orchard Books Australia
Level 17/207 Kent Street, Sydney, NSW 2000
A Paperback Original

First published in 2011 by Orchard Books

HiT entertainment

Illustrations © Orchard Books 2011

A CIP catalogue record for this book is available
from the British Library.

ISBN 978 1 40831 297 1

5 7 9 10 8 6 4

Printed in Great Britain

The paper and board used in this paperback are natural recyclable
products made from wood grown in sustainable forests. The
manufacturing processes conform to the environmental regulations
of the country of origin.

Orchard Books is a division of Hachette Children's Books,
an Hachette UK company

www.hachette.co.uk

Lizzie
the Sweet Treats
Fairy

by Daisy Meadows

ORCHARD

www.rainbowmagic.co.uk

The Fairyland Palace

The Orangery

The Lake

Maze

Petting Zoo

Topiary Garden

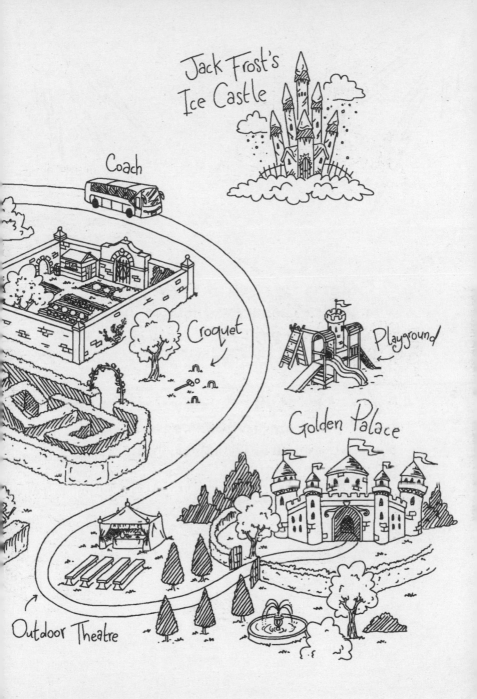

The fairies are planning a magical ball,
With guests of honour and fun for them all.
They're expecting a night full of laughter and cheer
But they'll get a shock when my goblins appear!

Adventures and treats will be things of the past,
And I'll beat those troublesome fairies at last.
My iciest magic will blast through the room
And the world will be plunged into grimness
and gloom!

Contents

Royal Tea Party

"Having a tea party here in the Orangery is going to be really fun!" Rachel Walker exclaimed to her best friend Kirsty Tate. "I bet that's just what the *real* princes and princesses who lived in Golden Palace used to do."

"I wonder if we're going to have a royal tea of cucumber sandwiches and cream cakes?" Kirsty agreed with a smile. "The Orangery is the perfect place for a special party!"

The Orangery was a gleaming white building with huge arched windows that stood in the grounds of Golden Palace. Terracotta pots of orange, lemon and lime trees lined the walls of the Orangery, and the air was warm

and scented with citrus smells. A spiral staircase in the middle of the building swept up to the wrought-iron balcony overhead, giving spectacular views out of the windows of Golden Palace and its enormous grounds. From the balcony Rachel and Kirsty could see the drawbridge and moat, the lake and ornamental gardens, the maze, the petting zoo and the croquet field.

"Golden Palace looks lovely in the sunshine," Kirsty remarked. The palace had four high towers, one at each corner of the building, and a fifth tower, the highest one, right in the centre. Flags flew on top of all five towers and their golden turrets glittered in the spring sun.

"Aren't we lucky to be here for Kids' Week?" Rachel beamed at Kirsty as

they made their way back down the
spiral staircase. "Thank you *so* much for
inviting me to come."

Golden Palace was located in the
countryside near Kirsty's home village of
Wetherbury, and the girls were spending
the spring holiday week there with a
group of other children, doing all sorts
of fun and interesting activities.

"Gather round, kids," called Louis,
one of the stewards who were looking
after the children during their holiday.
"Caroline and I are going to show you
how to lay the table for a tea party fit
for a prince or a princess!"

Rachel and Kirsty hurried over to
join the others. The ground floor of the
Orangery was laid out with tables and
chairs, ready for the tea party.

"Right, the first things we need are snowy-white tablecloths," Louis announced. Rachel, Kirsty and the others watched as he and Caroline shook out a heavy linen tablecloth and placed it on one of the tables, smoothing it down into place.

"And now for the matching napkins," Caroline said with a smile. She took one of the napkins and, with several swift folds, turned it into a fan. She folded the second napkin into a pretty flower shape, and the children laughed and applauded.

"That looks complicated!" Rachel whispered to Kirsty with a grin. Louis and Caroline added gleaming silver cutlery and floral china plates, dishes, teacups and saucers to the table, as well as a tiered cake-stand. The finishing touch was a little glass vase containing a single pink rose.

"Oh, this all looks gorgeous!" Rachel sighed. "I can just imagine a princess holding a tea party here, wearing her most beautiful gown."

"Don't forget we might meet a *fairy* princess today, Rachel!" Kirsty whispered in her ear.

All week long the girls had been helping their new friends, the Princess Fairies, search for their magical tiaras. On the day they'd arrived at Golden Palace, Rachel and Kirsty had been thrilled to receive an invitation to attend a Fairyland ball. But the ball had been ruined by Jack Frost and his goblins who had gatecrashed the party and stolen the Princess Fairies' tiaras, taking them away into the human world. But in the nick of time Queen Titania's magic spell had made sure that the tiaras would end up somewhere in Golden Palace so that the girls could help their fairy friends to find them and take them back to Fairyland.

"OK, now it's your turn, guys," Louis called. "Everything you need is on those side tables by the windows."

Rachel and Kirsty went to collect a tablecloth and some napkins. Then they began to lay their table, as did everyone else.

"I know we've found four of the magic tiaras so far," Rachel said in a low voice as she and Kirsty spread out the tablecloth. "But it's just *so* important that we find them all."

Kirsty nodded solemnly. Both girls knew that the Princess Fairies didn't just need their tiaras to look after their own special responsibility – the tiaras also affected *all* fairy magic. And without them no one in either the fairy or the human worlds would ever have a happy or magical time again.

Caroline came over and showed Rachel and Kirsty how to make flower and fan shapes from their napkins. Then the girls carefully laid out their china and cutlery.

"There!" Kirsty placed a little vase containing a white rose on the table and stood back to admire it. "What do you think, Rachel?"

17

"It looks great," Rachel said, "But let's give the cutlery another polish to make it really gleam."

She glanced around and spotted some cloths on one of the side tables next to a display of silver serving dishes. Then to Rachel's surprise, she noticed that one of the serving dishes was sparkling extra brightly in the sunshine that streamed through the arched windows.

"Kirsty!" Rachel tugged gently at her friend's arm. "Look over there. See that serving dish?"

"I see it!" Kirsty whispered excitedly. "Could that bright sparkle be fairy magic?"

"Let's find out!" Rachel replied.

The girls hurried over to the serving dish and stood in front of it so that no-one else could see. Then Rachel lifted the domed lid. And there on the silver tray sat a tiny fairy.

"It's Princess Lizzie the Sweet Treats Fairy!" Kirsty gasped.

Roses and Cupcakes

Lizzie jumped to her feet and waved up at the girls. She wore a bright yellow dress with a pink underskirt and strappy pink sandals. But she was dusted from head to toe with what looked like icing sugar and flour.

"Hello, girls," Lizzie whispered, a big smile on her face. "I was hoping you'd find me!"

"Why are
you so dusty,
Lizzie?" asked
Rachel as
the little fairy
brushed down
her clothes.

"I've been in
the palace kitchen
searching for my tiara," Lizzie explained.
"I'm sure it's there *somewhere*! Will you
help me look? Otherwise you won't have
any wonderful sweet treats for your tea
party."

"Of course we'll help," Kirsty told her.

At that moment Caroline clapped her
hands to get everyone's attention. Rachel
and Kirsty turned to look, shielding Lizzie
from sight.

"Louis and I think all your tables are great," Caroline announced. "The Orangery looks beautiful. And now it's time to prepare the food ready for the tea party so we're going over to the palace kitchen."

"But first you need *these*," Louis added, and he and Caroline began handing out white chef's hats and aprons.

"Good, we're going to the kitchen!" Kirsty murmured to Rachel as they dressed up in their hats and aprons. "That means we'll be able to look for Lizzie's tiara."

"Hurrah!" Lizzie exclaimed, looking excited. She dived into the pocket of Rachel's apron and ducked down out of sight.

Then Louis and Caroline led the way out of the Orangery towards the kitchen door at the back of Golden Palace. Rachel and Kirsty followed along with everyone else. But just as Caroline was about to pull the back door open, they all heard a loud wail of disappointment from inside.

"Oh, no! That wasn't supposed to happen!"

Wondering what was going on, everyone, including the girls, rushed into the kitchen. There they found Mrs King, the kindly palace cook, gazing down miserably at the cake tin she was holding. Inside was what looked like a pancake.

"Are you all right, Mrs King?" asked Louis.

Mrs King shook her head. "This is supposed to be a chocolate soufflé," she explained, "But look!" She held out the cake tin. "It's supposed to have risen in the oven – but it's as flat as when I put it in.

And the jelly hasn't set either." Mrs King pointed to a bowl of watery red goo on the worktop. "Nothing's going right today."

Kirsty and Rachel exchanged a glance. This was all because Lizzie's tiara was missing!

"Oh, poor Mrs King," said Caroline, patting the flustered cook on the arm. "But *something* smells delicious. What is it?"

Mrs King brightened a little as she pointed to rows of cupcakes sitting on cooling racks on the big pine table.

"The cupcakes have come out well, at least," she replied. "We'll be able to decorate them for the tea party."

"Lizzie's tiara couldn't have been far away when the cupcakes were baked if they've turned out OK!" Kirsty whispered to Rachel who nodded.

Everyone sat down at the table while Mrs King gave each pair of children a job to do. Some of them would be mixing different colours of icing and some would be making sugar flowers while others decorated the iced cakes.

As they waited their turn, Rachel and Kirsty stared around the kitchen, hoping to spot the tell-tale gleam of Lizzie's magic tiara. There were mixing-bowls, wooden spoons and baking tins on the work-tops, and tea trolleys were lined up against one of the walls, ready for the party. The door to the pantry stood open and inside were lots of jars and tins on shelves and big sacks of sugar and flour on the floor. But they couldn't see the missing tiara anywhere.

"Kirsty and Rachel, you'll be making crystallised rose petals," Mrs King announced with a smile. "We'll put them on the cakes and scatter them on the cake stands, too."

"Oh, that sounds lovely!" said Kirsty.

Mrs King handed Rachel a little basket. "That's the way to the kitchen garden," the cook told the girls, pointing to a door on the other side of the room. "You'll find the rose bushes at the bottom of the garden, past the vegetables. Collect as many different-coloured petals as you can, and then we'll paint them with egg-white and dust them with sugar."

"They're going to look so pretty!" Rachel remarked as she and Kirsty went out of the door.

The kitchen garden was neatly laid out and packed with young vegetable plants, rows of herbs and sweet-scented lavender shrubs. In one corner was a shed with the door open, revealing a collection of gardening tools.

"It smells gorgeous out here," said Kirsty, sniffing the air.

"Look, there are the roses," Rachel pointed out.

The roses were scrambling up some

tall trellises at the bottom of the kitchen
garden. They were covered with fragrant
white, pink and pale yellow blooms,
and the girls stopped to admire them
for a moment.

"Let's just take one or two petals
from some of the flowers,"
Kirsty suggested. "It
seems a shame to
pick a whole
bloom when they
look so lovely
growing here."

Rachel nodded
as Lizzie fluttered
out of her apron
pocket and hovered
over the roses.

"I'll help, girls!" Lizzie cried.

Rachel and Kirsty set to work carefully plucking a petal here and a petal there. Meanwhile Lizzie sat in the basket and sorted them into different colours, stacking the petals neatly.

As the girls were working, Kirsty suddenly became aware of gruff voices on the other side of the trellis. She nudged Rachel.

"Who's that?" she asked.

"It might be the gardeners," Rachel replied.

Kirsty stepped up to the trellis, parted the prickly branches of the rose and peered through the wooden slats. Her eyes widened as she saw three goblins! They were also dressed in chef's hats and aprons, and they were digging a large and very messy hole.

Beside the goblins was a wheelbarrow
full of grass clippings and leaves. Kirsty
guessed that the gardeners must have
left it behind.

Then Kirsty clapped her hand to her
mouth in excitement. She'd just spotted
Lizzie's missing golden
tiara underneath
the wheelbarrow!
It was leaning
against one of
the wheels and
twinkling brightly
in the spring sunshine.

"What is it, Kirsty?" asked Rachel.

"There are three goblins behind the
trellis, and they have Lizzie's tiara!"
Kirsty gasped.

Lizzie in a Tizzy!

Rachel and Lizzie rushed to look.
They could see the tiara glittering and
gleaming in the sunshine.

"This is a brilliant hiding-place,"
the biggest goblin panted as he tossed
another shovelful of earth aside.
"No-one will ever guess the tiara's
buried in the ground."

"It was *my* idea to bury the tiara," one of the other goblins boasted.

"No, it wasn't," the third retorted crossly, "It was *my* idea!"

"We must get the tiara back," Rachel whispered to Lizzie and Kirsty under cover of the goblins' bickering. "But we can't reach it from here."

Suddenly Kirsty remembered the garden shed they'd seen earlier. "I have an idea," she whispered to Rachel and Lizzie. "Wait here!"

Kirsty hurried over to the shed, went inside and saw exactly what she was looking for – a rake. Quickly she grabbed it and then dashed back to Rachel and Lizzie. Kneeling down on their side of the trellis, Kirsty poked the head of the rake through the slats and out the other side.

"Good thinking, Kirsty!" Rachel murmured.

Kirsty carefully moved the rake backwards and forwards, trying to hook the tiara onto its teeth. But as she was doing so, the rake nudged the wheelbarrow wheel, sending the barrow rolling forwards slightly.

Kirsty froze as the goblins stopped digging and turned around.

"That's strange," the biggest goblin remarked.

"The wind must have moved it," said one of the others.

Then they all started shovelling again. Kirsty breathed a sigh of relief. She tried once more, and this time she managed to snare the tiara. As quietly as she could, she began to drag the tiara towards the trellis.

Suddenly, though, the tiara got stuck on a rose root. Kirsty muffled an exclamation of dismay and tugged at the rake, trying to free the tiara, but it wouldn't budge. Rachel slid her arm between the slats and tried to grab it, but it wasn't close enough.

"I'll get it, girls," Lizzie whispered.

Rachel and Kirsty watched as Lizzie fluttered through the slats of the trellis.

"The hole should be big enough now," one of the goblins declared, throwing aside his spade. "Let's get the tiara."

The girls glanced at each other
anxiously as the goblins turned to
the wheelbarrow.

"It's gone!" the biggest goblin yelled.
"No, there it is!" the third goblin
shouted, pointing at
the tiara stuck on
the rose root.
"And there's
a pesky fairy
after it, too!"
"Quick,
we must help
Lizzie!" Rachel
said urgently to Kirsty.
The girls dashed around the
trellis and were just in time to see the
goblins upending the wheelbarrow
as Lizzie hovered around the tiara.

The leaves and grass clippings tumbled out of the barrow and fell on top of the little fairy, completely covering her.

"We need to find another hiding-place," the big goblin yelled, grabbing the tiara, "And fast!"

As the goblins ran off, Kirsty and Rachel rushed to pull Lizzie out of the pile of leaves and grass.

"Oh, thank you, girls!" Lizzie gasped, shaking a leaf from her hair. "What shall we do now? I'm so worried I may never get my beautiful tiara back."

"We won't give up, Lizzie," Rachel replied in a determined voice. "The goblins can't have gone far."

"Maybe we'd better take these rose petals back to Mrs King," Kirsty suggested. "Then we can think about where we're going to look next."

Lizzie flew to hide in Rachel's apron pocket and Kirsty retrieved the basket of rose petals. Then they headed back to the kitchen. But when they arrived, the girls couldn't believe their eyes. The three goblins were sitting at the table along with everyone else, and they were mixing up an enormous bowl of green icing!

What a Mess!

"Ah, there you are, girls," said Mrs King. "Come and sit down. Wash the rose petals carefully, please, and then you can crystallise them."

Rachel and Kirsty hurried to sit down next to the goblins, hoping they might find out where they'd hidden Lizzie's tiara this time. The goblins were giggling away and having a great time.

Their faces were smeared with crumbs
because when they thought no one was
looking, they kept taking one sneaky
bite out of each of the delicious cupcakes
in front of them. Then they rearranged
the cakes on the cooling racks so that
Mrs King wouldn't notice.

"Look at me!" said
the biggest goblin.
He stuck his
hand into the
bowl and drew
a green icing
moustache
on his face.
The other
two goblins
roared with
laughter.

Then one of the
others pulled out
a lump of icing
and made
himself two
long green
earrings which
he hung from
his big ears.
They all laughed
even harder.

"I wish we knew what they've done
with Lizzie's tiara," Rachel murmured
to Kirsty. The girls had finished washing
the petals and were now coating them
with egg-white. They were trying to
keep a sharp eye on the goblins, but it
was difficult when they had their own
job to be getting on with.

Kirsty took a quick glance at the goblins and couldn't help but grin. "Look what they're doing with their cupcakes, Rachel!" she whispered.

Instead of icing their cupcakes separately, the goblins had stuck all the little cakes together in a heap and they were now covering them with thick green icing to make one lop-sided giant blob of a cake.

"What a mess!" Rachel said, frowning as one of the goblins ran his finger around the mixing bowl and licked the icing off.

Kirsty saw Lizzie peeping out of Rachel's pocket and looking rather worried. "No sign of your tiara yet, Lizzie," Kirsty whispered as she and Rachel dipped their petals into a bowl of sugar. "But we'll keep looking."

Soon everyone had finished their preparations. Then Mrs King, Louis and Caroline helped everyone to decorate the cupcakes with icing, silver balls, sugar flowers and Rachel and Kirsty's crystallised rose petals. The little cakes looked beautiful when they'd finished.

"It's time to take the cakes over to the Orangery now," said Mrs King, glancing at the clock. "The tea party will be starting soon, so we'd better load everything onto the trolley. You've all worked very hard and the cakes are looking wonderful!"

Rachel and Kirsty carried their cupcakes over to the trolley and so did everyone else except the goblins. They were fighting over the mixing bowl to scoop out the leftover icing.

"Well, this is a rather – er - unusual cake," Mrs King said, staring at the big messy green blob in front of the goblins. She picked the cake up and placed it on an empty trolley.

"No!" the biggest goblin yelled. He jumped up and stamped his foot furiously, grabbing hold of the trolley handle. "You *can't* take our cake – it's a special cake with a special surprise in it!"

Rachel's eyes widened as she realised what the goblin meant. "I can guess *exactly* what the special surprise is," Rachel whispered to Kirsty. "The goblins have hidden Lizzie's tiara in their cake!"

Trolley Dash!

Kirsty nodded. "They must have put the tiara in among the cupcakes and then quickly covered it with icing when we weren't looking!" she whispered back. "We can't let Mrs King take it to the Orangery."

Rachel hurried over to the cook. "Maybe the boys think their cake needs a bit more work," she suggested.

"Kirsty and I could help them finish off, and then we can bring it over to the Orangery in a little while."

"That's a good idea," Mrs King agreed. "Come along then, the rest of you. Let's wheel these trolleys over to the Orangery."

Rachel and Kirsty waited as Louis and Caroline held open the kitchen doors and everyone followed Mrs King out, wheeling their trolleys along with them. Now the only trolley left in the kitchen was the one with the goblins' green cake on it.

The goblins were still grabbing the mixing bowl from each other and trying to scrape out the  last bits of icing for themselves. They didn't even notice that everyone else had left the kitchen except for Rachel and Kirsty.

"Good work, girls," Lizzie called, flying out of the pocket of Rachel's apron. "And now let's get my tiara back!" She zoomed over to the goblins who shrieked with rage as they spotted her.

"We know where you've hidden my tiara," Lizzie said, "And we'd like it back, please."

"No way!" yelled the biggest goblin. The three of them jumped up from their chairs and ran off across the kitchen, taking the trolley with the cake on it with them.

"Help me catch them, girls!" Lizzie cried, whizzing around Rachel and Kirsty and showering them with fairy magic from her wand. Instantly the girls shrank down to fairy-size, and fluttering their glittering wings, the three friends gave chase.

The goblins were careering crazily around the enormous kitchen with the trolley. They were bumping into everything as they raced about, setting all the copper pots and pans hanging on the walls rattling loudly. Then they banged into the table, knocking over

some of the chairs as well as a bowl
of pink icing. The bowl crashed to the
floor, spilling icing everywhere. Even
though Lizzie and the girls did their best
to catch up with the goblins by darting
here and there, they didn't have a
chance of retrieving the tiara.

"Keep moving!" the biggest goblin shouted to the other two. "Those pesky fairies can't do a thing if we keep on running, ha ha ha!"

"He's right," Kirsty panted, "We're just flying around in circles! How are we going to stop them?"

Lizzie was hovering above the spilt pink icing on the kitchen floor. She stared down at it thoughtfully.

"We've seen how greedy the goblins are," Lizzie said, "They love the icing and the cakes. Maybe we can use that to stop them and get my tiara back."

She flew down to the table and pointed
at one of the piping bags that had been
filled with icing to decorate the cupcakes.
"Give me a hand, please, Rachel!"

Rachel and Lizzie lifted up the bag
between them and waited for the goblins
to pass by with the trolley. Then they
aimed the bag at the
biggest goblin
and pressed
down
hard. Pale
blue icing
squirted
out of the
bag and hit
the goblin
right in the
face.

"Stop that!" the goblin roared. But then he licked a little bit of the icing off with his tongue. "Lovely" he said,

stopping to lick *all* the icing off his face.

Meanwhile Kirsty had spotted a jar of silver balls open on the table. She waited until the remaining two goblins dashed past with the trolley, then she tipped the jar over. The balls cascaded over the floor.

"What's happening?" the second goblin squealed as he slithered about on the

silver balls. "The floor's all slippery!" He
tried desperately to regain his balance but
only ended up on
his bottom.

  Now
there was
only one
goblin left
whizzing
the trolley
around the
kitchen. Rachel
wondered how to stop
him, but then she remembered how the
goblins had covered Lizzie with the leaves
and grass from the wheelbarrow. That
gave her an idea. She swooped down
towards the trolley and managed to grab
a lump of sponge from the green cake as

the goblin sped towards her.

"Look, I have yummy cake!" Rachel called, waving it in front of the goblin's nose. "Would you like it? Or shall I eat it myself?"

"Give it to me!" the goblin demanded, licking his lips.

"Come and get it then," Rachel replied. She flew over to the pantry and through the open door where she hovered above the sacks of flour and sugar that lay on the floor. The goblin raced into the pantry after her, his eyes fixed greedily on the piece of cake Rachel was holding. At the last possible moment Rachel zoomed up into the air out of reach and the goblin crashed the trolley straight into the sacks, splitting them open. A large white cloud of

flour-dust rose up into the air.

"I can't see a thing!" the goblin complained, coughing and spluttering. "Where's that fairy gone with my cake?"

"Well done, girls!" Lizzie cried. "And now to find my tiara!"

A Magical Cake

Lizzie swooped down and picked up a spoon from the table. Rachel and Kirsty did the same. Then the three of them fluttered over to the cake on the trolley and, using the spoons like shovels, they began to dig through the gloopy green icing and lumps of sponge.

Suddenly Kirsty spotted something glittering brightly beneath the cupcakes.

"I can see the tiara!" she exclaimed, digging away with her spoon.

A few moments later all the sponge and icing had been scraped away and Lizzie's golden tiara was revealed.

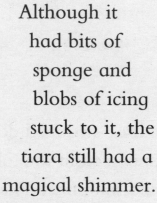

Although it had bits of sponge and blobs of icing stuck to it, the tiara still had a magical shimmer.

Rachel and Kirsty beamed at each other in delight.

"I'm so happy I have my tiara back!" Lizzie sighed. With one whisk of her wand she quickly cleaned the tiara and it shrank down to its fairy size.

Lizzie picked it up carefully and placed it on her head while Rachel and Kirsty clapped and cheered.

"We've lost the tiara!" grumbled the biggest goblin, "And now I feel sick, too!"

"Me, too," the second goblin agreed, "My tummy aches!"

"We ate too many sweet treats," the third goblin groaned, holding his stomach. Complaining loudly, all three goblins stomped off outside.

Lizzie, Rachel and Kirsty couldn't help laughing.

"Maybe they won't be so greedy next time!" Rachel remarked.

"Girls, I can't thank you enough," Lizzie cried. "I can't wait to get back to Fairyland and tell everyone how clever you've been. But first —" she glanced around the kitchen — "we'd better clean up this mess."

Another flick of Lizzie's wand, and Rachel and Kirsty were restored to their human size.

Quickly Kirsty picked up
the chairs the goblins
had knocked over
while Rachel
found a broom
to sweep up
the silver balls.
Meanwhile
Lizzie's fairy
magic cleared
up all the spilt
icing and clouds
of flour. Soon the
kitchen was spick and span.

"What are we going to do about the
goblins' cake?" Kirsty said, staring at the
mess of sponge and icing on the trolley.
"We told Mrs King we'd take it over to
the Orangery."

Lizzie smiled. She flew to hover over the cake and let a stream of fairy sparkles fall onto it from her wand. The goblins' green sponge vanished and in its place was an amazing golden-coloured, palace-shaped cake with five towers.

"It's Golden Palace!" Rachel exclaimed with delight. "Look, Kirsty, the towers even have little paper flags on top of them."

"It's gorgeous!" Kirsty gasped.

"Enjoy your tea party, girls," Lizzie said with a smile. "Goodbye, and thank you once again." Then she disappeared in a haze of fairy dust.

Rachel and Kirsty wheeled the trolley with the Golden Palace cake on it over to the Orangery where the tea party had already started.

Everyone was sitting at the tables and a buzz of excited chatter filled the air.

"Ah, there you are, girls," said Mrs King, coming to meet them. "Didn't the boys want to come to the party?"

Rachel shook her head. "No, they said they'd had too many sweet treats already!" she replied.

"Well, everyone here is loving your rose petal decorations," Mrs King told them. Then she noticed the cake and her eyes widened in amazement. "Goodness me, girls, that's wonderful!" Mrs King declared. "A Golden Palace cake! I don't think I could have done better myself. You two certainly have a magic touch!"

Rachel and Kirsty laughed, and exchanged a secret smile.

"Five fairy tiaras found," Kirsty whispered. "And two to go!"

Now it's time for Kirsty and
Rachel to help...

Maddie the Playtime Fairy

Read on for a sneak peek...

"I've never seen such beautiful toys!"
gasped Rachel Walker, gazing around
with wide eyes.

"I can imagine the princes and
princesses playing with them long
ago," agreed her best friend Kirsty Tate
dreamily.

The girls were standing in the Royal
Nursery at the top of Golden Palace,
where they were staying for a special
'Kids' Week'. The other children were
already kneeling down beside the toys,
choosing what they wanted to play with.

There was a model steam engine that ran along a track around the room, a large jar full of swirly glass marbles, and boxes filled with skittles and wooden spinning tops. Pretty china dolls sat on low shelves beside plump teddy bears, and balls of every size and colour rolled around their feet.

"Oh Rachel, look!" cried Kirsty.

On a low table in one corner of the room stood an exact miniature copy of Golden Palace. It had the same gleaming white stone walls and golden turrets. Tiny flags fluttered from the battlements.

Rachel and Kirsty carefully opened the front wall to look inside. The rooms were exactly the same as those in the real palace, with thick carpets and plush furniture. There were dolls dressed in royal robes, as well as maids and butlers.

"This must be the princess," said Rachel, picking up a tiny girl doll with flowing golden hair and a sparkling tiara.

"She reminds me of Lizzie the Sweet Treats Fairy," whispered Kirsty.

The girls smiled at each other, thinking about their wonderful secret. They were good friends of the fairies, and often had magical adventures in Fairyland...

Read Maddie the Playtime Fairy to find out what adventures are in store for Kirsty and Rachel!

Meet the Sweet Fairies

If Kirsty and Rachel don't find
the Sweet Fairies' magical charms,
Jack Frost will ruin all sweet treats for ever!

www.rainbowmagicbooks.co.uk

Meet the fairies, play games
and get sneak peeks at
the latest books!

www.rainbowmagicbooks.co.uk

There's fairy fun for everyone on
our wonderful website.
You'll find great activities, competitions, stories and
fairy profiles, and also a special newsletter.

Get 30% off all Rainbow Magic books at

www.rainbowmagicbooks.co.uk

Enter the code RAINBOW at the checkout.
Offer ends 31 December 2013.

Offer valid in United Kingdom and Republic of Ireland only.

Nicki the Holiday Camp Fairy

Rachel and Kirsty have been looking forward to camp, but everything is going wrong. Can they help Nicki fix things, before the whole summer is ruined?

www.rainbowmagicbooks.co.uk

Alexandra the Royal Baby Fairy

The whole of Fairyland is very excited - there's going to be a new royal baby! But when the special baby goes missing, Rachel and Kirsty are there to help their friend, Alexandra the Royal Baby Fairy.

www.rainbowmagicbooks.co.uk